Bring the Classics to Life

The Christmas Carol

LEVEL 1

Series Designer
Philip J. Solimene

Editor
Janice Cobas

Black & White Illustrations
Ken Landgraf

EDCON PUBLISHING

New York

Story Adaptor
Rachel Armington

Author
Charles Dickens

About the Author

Charles Dickens was born in the year 1812 in England. Reading, music, and theater were important to his family. When he was 12 years old, his parents sent him to work in a factory. His family was sent to debtor's prison soon after that. Charles was on his own for several months. After this time in his life he always cared deeply for the homeless and the hungry. In his articles and his books, Dickens often wrote about the laws that pushed people deeper and deeper into poverty. One reason Dickens wrote *A Christmas Carol* was to encourage people to help the poor. Some of Dickens's other well known books are *Oliver Twist, David Copperfield, A Tale of Two Cities*, and *Great Expectations.*

info@edconpublishing.com
1-888-553-3266   Fax 1-888-518-1564
30 Montauk Blvd. Oakdale NY 11769
www.edconpublishing.com

Printed in U.S.A.
10 ISBN #1-55576-557-2
13 ISBN #978-1-55576-557-6

CONTENTS

WORDS USED

	Key Words	**Necessary Words**
Story 91	alone are give his money there	borrow Christmas count family nephew poor
Story 92	door hear friend walk was why	believe chains close dead ghost through
Story 93	next night one three when window	bell crowd end hide ring suffer
Story 94	am boy girl light man school	change dance heart remember touch wrong
Story 95	be cry her laugh more woman	afraid face love marry push world

WORDS USED

	Key Words	**Necessary Words**
Story 96	over many never room street than	brothers cook food seen sprinkle torch
Story 97	as every from live people us	bless crutch goose held song wife
Story 98	ask does happy old they your	beware float himself hurt robe should
Story 99	bed black take thing time who	bury care fell pointed sheet shirt
Story 100	after all day hand hurry if	clothes crazy future grave need sorry

Alone for Christmas

PREPARATION

Key Words

alone	(ə lōn´)	by oneself, or away from other people *Mom and Dad do not want me to walk home <u>alone</u>.*
are	(är)	a form of the verb "to be": *We <u>are</u> going to play at my house.*
give	(giv)	to let someone have *Mary did not want to <u>give</u> the toys away.*
his	(hiz)	belonging to a boy or a man *Daddy did not want my dog to ride in <u>his</u> car.*
money	(mun´ ē)	special pieces of paper or metal used to buy or sell *Angie is making <u>money</u> for a new bike.*
there	(T͟Hâr)	in, at, or to that place *My friend wants me to come <u>there</u> now.*
		"there" is sometimes used at the beginning of a sentence *<u>There</u> are ways to help your mother.*

Alone for Christmas

Necessary Words

borrow (bor´ ō) to take something with the promise to give it back later
I wanted to <u>borrow</u> his toy airplane, but he said "no."

Christmas (kris´ mə s) December 25: on this day many people celebrate the birth of Christ, who taught that people should be gentle and kind to each other
On <u>Christmas</u> we try to help people who do not have as much as we do.

count (kount) to find out how many there are of something
Can you <u>count</u> the books in your house?

family (fam´ə lē) a child or group of children who have a father and mother
Josh is happy Grandmom is coming to live with his <u>family</u>. Many families like to take walks together.

nephew (nef´ yü) the son of one's brother or sister
My <u>nephew</u> wants to come to play at my house.

poor (pu̇r) having very little
The <u>poor</u> family did not have money to buy a home.
The people who are poor
The <u>poor</u> get cold when it snows.

People, Places, and Things

Bah! Humbug! is what Scrooge says to show he does not believe something. A "humbug" is a silly trick or something not true.

Christmas Eve is the night before Christmas.

Counting house is a business that keeps track of who has given and who has borrowed money. Scrooge lets people borrow money from him, but they have to pay back much more than they borrowed.

Gentleman is a man who does not have to work for a living.

Prison in this story is a debtor's prison. If someone did not pay back money he borrowed, he and his family would be locked up until he could pay. Because they were locked up and could not work, some families never got out.

Workhouse is a place where poor people lived. When a family came into a workhouse, the mother, father, boys and girls were all kept apart from each other. They were given very little food and long hours of hard work. Some poor people chose to die rather than go into a workhouse.

7

Alone for Christmas

Scrooge's nephew comes to see him on Christmas Eve.

Preview
1. Read the name of the story.
2. Look at the picture.
3. Read the sentence under the picture.
4. Read the first (   ) paragraphs of the story.
5. Then answer the following question.

You learned from your preview that Scrooge
    ____a. is very friendly.
    ____b. likes to work with money
    ____c. wants his nephew to come work for him.
    ____d. likes to give money to Bob Cratchit.

Turn to the Comprehension Check on page 10 for the right answer.

Now read the story.
Read to find out what Scrooge wants to do on Christmas day.

8

Alone for Christmas

Ebenezer Scrooge liked to count money. He did not like Christmas.

Scrooge worked at his counting house. Bob Cratchit worked for Scrooge for a little money. Scrooge did not like to give Bob money for his work. "Bob's family is big," said Scrooge. "His big family is what makes Bob poor, not me."

On Christmas Eve, Scrooge looked up to see his nephew come in. A good Christmas to you!" said his nephew.

"Bah!" said Scrooge. "Humbug!"

"Christmas is not a humbug!" said his nephew.

"What good is Christmas?" said Scrooge. "Christmas will not make me money!"

"What good is money?" said his nephew. "Money is the humbug! This Christmas will give you something money can not give you. You will see!"

"I like Christmas," said Bob Cratchit.

"I like to see you work!" said Scrooge. Bob Cratchit jumped. He looked down at his work.

"Now, Fred, what do you want?" Scrooge said to his nephew. "Did you come to borrow money?"

"My family is not poor. I do not have to borrow money," said Fred. "I want you to stop counting money for now. Come to my house. My family wants to see you there. I do not want to see you alone on Christmas."

"I do not want to see you on Christmas," said Scrooge. "I will have my Christmas alone. Now, go away, nephew!"

Bob Cratchit worked. Scrooge counted money. He looked up to see a gentleman come in the counting house.

"What do you want?" Scrooge said. "Do you want to borrow money?"

"I do not want to borrow money. I want you to help me get money to poor families," said the gentleman. "Will you give money to the poor this Christmas?"

"You want me to give money to the poor? I do not have to help," said Scrooge. "Are there no prisons?"

"You can not want the poor to go to prison!" said the gentleman.

"Are there no workhouses?" said Scrooge.

"The poor do not want to go to the workhouse!" said the gentleman. "A little money can give a poor family a home for Christmas."

"I work to make my money," said Scrooge. "I do not work to give my money away!"

"Go and look at the poor families," said the gentleman. "You will want to help!"

"Bah! I do not want to help!" said Scrooge. "The poor will not get my money! I want my money for me! I do not want to have to look at the poor. I want the poor to go away. I want you to go away!"

Alone for Christmas

COMPREHENSION CHECK

Choose the best answer.

1. Bob Cratchit is
____a.   Scrooge's nephew.
____b.   Scrooge's friend.
____c.   coming to borrow money.
____d.   a man who works for Scrooge.

2. Bob Cratchit is poor because
____a.   Bob's children have too many toys.
____b.   the counting house does not make any money.
____c.   Scrooge does not pay him very much.
____d.   Bob's family lives in a big house.

3. Scrooge calls Christmas a "humbug"
____a.   to stop Fred from asking him for money.
____b.   to warn his nephew about bugs on the floor.
____c.   so that Bob Cratchit will keep working.
____d.   because he doesn't think Christmas is worth anything.

4. When Fred comes to the counting house he
____a.   asks Scrooge to come to his house for Christmas.
____b.   asks to borrow money.
____c.   tells Bob Cratchit to jump.
____d.   asks if his family can come to Scrooge's house.

5. Two people come to the counting house to see Scrooge. They are
____a.   Bob Cratchit and Fred.
____b.   Fred and the gentleman.
____c.   Bob Cratchit and the gentleman.
____d.   The gentleman and the humbug.

6. When the gentleman comes to the counting house
____a.   Scrooge gives him money.
____b.   he wants Scrooge to come with him.
____c.   he wants to borrow money.
____d.   he wants Scrooge to help the poor.

7. Scrooge works so that he
____a.   has a nice home.
____b.   has money to help Fred with his big family.
____c.   can have more money for himself.
____d.   has enough money to move away from people.

8. Scrooge says he wants
____a.   the poor to go away so he does not have to look at them.
____b.   to make more money than the gentleman.
____c.   the gentleman to help Bob Cratchit's family.
____d.   to have Fred come back after Christmas.

9. Another name for this story could be
____a.   "Scrooge Makes a New Friend."
____b.   "Fred Has a Party."
____c.   "Christmas Eve at the Counting House."
____d.   "The Poor Come to Scrooge."

10. This story is mainly about
____a.   people who should give money to the poor.
____b.   how Scrooge wants to be alone with his money.
____c.   a gentleman who gives money to the poor.
____d.   how Fred wants Scrooge to see his family.

Check your answers with the keys on page 67.

Alone for Christmas

VOCABULARY CHECK

alone	are	give	his	money	there

I. Sentences to Finish
Fill in the blank in each sentence with the correct key word from the box above.

1. My mother is working to make _____ for a car.

2. Will you _____ the red ball to me?

3. What _____ you looking for?

4. Stop jumping up and down over _____!

5. "It is not fun to play _____," Pam said to her mother.

6. Allan makes _____ toy cars go fast!

II. Making Sense of Sentences
Put a check next to YES if the sentence makes sense. Put a check next to NO if the sentence does not make sense.

1. I <u>are</u> happy to go with you. ____YES ____NO

2. Stan said we can come in <u>his</u> car. ____YES ____NO

3. <u>Money</u> is blue and runs like a cat. ____YES ____NO

4. I want Mick, Ann, and John to come with me so I can be <u>alone</u>. ____YES ____NO

5. I do not want to go <u>there</u> with you. ____YES ____NO

6. <u>Give</u> me the ball, and we can play. ____YES ____NO

Check your answers with the keys on page 68.
This page may be reproduced for classroom use.

Marley's Ghost

PREPARATION

Key Words

door	(dôr)	something that can be opened or closed to block off a gap in a wall *My family has gone in and out of the <u>door</u> all day.*
hear	(hir)	to take in sound through one's ears *Speak louder! I can not <u>hear</u> you!*
friend	(frend)	a person who one likes and enjoys being with *My <u>friend</u> said something very funny today.*
walk	(wȯk)	to move by one's feet *I had to <u>walk</u> home in the rain.*
was	(wuz)	a form of "to be" that shows what happened in the past *Jenna <u>was</u> jumping up and down when I came in.*
why	(hwī)	for what reason *<u>Why</u> did Dylan give you his toys?*

Marley's Ghost

Necessary Words

believe   (bi lēv´)   to think something is true
I believe you will do the best work you can.
to think something really exists
Do you believe there are monsters under the bed?

chains   (chānz)   a row of metal rings joined one to the other
The king put the thief in chains so he could not get away.

close   (klōz)   to block the way in or the way out; to shut
Rick did not close the gate to stop the pig from running out.

dead   (ded)   no longer living
Mother was sad to find a dead bird in the garden.

ghost   (gōst)   the form or shape of a dead person which living people can sometimes see
Nat was alone in the dark house when he saw the ghost!

through   (thrü)   from one end or side to the other
Do not run through the house when father is sleeping.

People, Places, and Things

A knocker   is made of metal and often has fancy decorations molded into it. A knocker is attached to the outside of a front door. The top part of the knocker is lifted and rapped down against the bottom part. A knocker makes a louder sound than knocking with one's hands.

Marley   owned the counting house with Scrooge. Every time he did something unkind, he added another ring to the chains he would have to carry when he was dead.

13

Marley's Ghost

Scrooge sees his friend Marley on the door's knocker!

Preview   1. Read the name of the story.
2. Look at the picture.
3. Read the sentence under the picture.
4. Read the first (   ) paragraphs of the story.
5. Then answer the following question.

You learned from your preview that Scrooge's friend Marley
_____a. will not work on Christmas.
_____b. is dead.
_____c. has come to stay at Scrooge's house.
_____d. likes Christmas.

Turn to the Comprehension Check on page 16 for the right answer.

Now read the story.
Read to find out what happens when Scrooge goes into his house.

14

Marley's Ghost

"You will not work on Christmas!" Scrooge said to Bob Cratchit. "Why do I have to give money to you for playing at home? This is why I do not like Christmas! You will have to make up the work!"

"I will," said Bob.

"Bah! You can close the counting house," Scrooge said. "I will walk home now."

At his house, Scrooge stopped at the door and looked up at the knocker. "Something is on the knocker," Scrooge said. "It looks like my friend Marley! Why do I see my friend now? Marley is dead! I can not believe this!"

Scrooge looked and looked at the knocker. He did not see Marley now. "This is humbug," said Scrooge. "Humbug!"

Scrooge walked in and closed the door. "I worked with Marley at his and my counting house. This house was Marley's. Now I have his house. This is why I was seeing Marley on the knocker!"

Closing doors, Scrooge walked through the big house. "I hear something!" said Scrooge. "I hear chains! It is said ghosts walk with chains. I do not believe in ghosts. A ghost can not be walking through my house!" Scrooge stopped. "What is this I hear coming up to my door?"

The closed door did not stop the Ghost. He walked through the door. The Ghost looked like Marley! Scrooge wanted to get away. He looked through the Ghost to his door. "I do not want to walk through a ghost! I can not get to the door!"

The Ghost looked down at Scrooge. Scrooge looked at the big chains on the Ghost. "You can not be my friend Marley," Scrooge said. "He is dead!"

"You do not believe in me," said the Ghost.

"I do not believe in ghosts," Scrooge said. "You are a humbug."

"You see and hear me," said the Ghost. "Why do you not believe in what you see and hear?"

Scrooge looked at the Ghost. "I believe it is you, Marley. Why have you come to me?"

"Ghosts like me want to do something good to help," said Marley. "We are dead. We are alone! We can not help!"

"Why do you have the chains on you?" said Scrooge.

"I was making my chains at the counting house. This is what I did to make my chains: I believed money was all I wanted. I did not want to help the poor. I did not see the chains I was making," said Marley. "You can not see the chains you are making now!"

Scrooge looked down. "I do believe I have chains I can not see! You are dead. Is this why you can see the chains on me, and I can not? Help me, Marley!"

Marley's Ghost

COMPREHENSION CHECK

Choose the best answer.

1. Scrooge does not like Christmas because
____a. he will have to give money to Bob for a day he does not work.
____b. Scrooge feels badly he does not have a family like Bob's.
____c. the counting house has a lot of work to do.
____d. Scrooge does not want to see Bob happy.

2. Scrooge believes he saw Marley on the knocker because
____a. Scrooge can not see very well.
____b. someone drew Marley's picture on the door.
____c. the house belonged to Marley first.
____d. Scrooge wishes his friend would come back.

3. Scrooge's house
____a. is next door to Fred's house.
____b. was Scrooge's until Marley gave him money for it.
____c. is big with a lot of doors to close.
____d. was where Scrooge lived as a boy.

4. When Scrooge sees the Ghost, he
____a. runs out of the house.
____b. tries to close the door on the Ghost.
____c. is happy to see Marley again.
____d. wants to get away.

5. Scrooge calls the Ghost a "Humbug"
____a. to scare the Ghost away.
____b. because he does not want to believe in ghosts.
____c. because he only believes in money.
____d. to trick the Ghost so Scrooge can run away.

6. Marley tells Scrooge that he wants
____a. to help the living.
____b. Scrooge to get out of his house.
____c. to be with people again.
____d. help getting his chains off.

7. Marley's chains came from
____a. wanting money and not helping the poor.
____b. ghosts of people he had tricked.
____c. the long life he lived.
____d. the prison he was living in.

8. Scrooge does not see the chains he is making because
____a. his chains are too little to see.
____b. the chains will go on him when he is dead.
____c. Marley is playing a trick on him.
____d. he is not dead so he can not see the ghostly chains.

9. Another name for this story could be
____a. "Walking Home."
____b. "The Door at Fred's House."
____c. "A Visit From a Friend."
____d. "Bob Cratchit Goes Home."

10. This story is mainly about
____a. Marley having chains.
____b. Scrooge seeing something that can not be true.
____c. Scrooge closing doors in his house.
____d. Scrooge coming to believe the Ghost is Marley.

Check your answers with the keys on page 67.
This page may be reproduced for classroom use.

16

Marley's Ghost

VOCABULARY CHECK

door	hear	friend	walk	was	why

I. Sentences to Finish
Fill in the blank in each sentence with the correct key word from the box above.

1. Billy likes to see how fast he can _____ .

2. Do not open the _____ or the cat will get out.

3. _____ do you want to come with me?

4. Todd wants his _____ to come play at his house.

5. The work _____ so hard I had to stop.

6. I can _____ my family playing in the house.

II. Mixed-up Words
First unscramble the words and write them in the spaces in Column A. Then match the keywords with the right sentences in Column B by drawing lines.

Column A   Column B

1. hyw _____   a. Did you _____ what I said?

2. aerh _____   b. I _____ going to come with you.

3. orod _____   c. Herb likes to play with his _____.

4. asw _____   d. Frances can not _____ as fast as her father.

5. dreifn _____   e. I like the red _____ on the house.

6. kwal _____   f. Mother said, "_____ do you
                             have to borrow money?"

Check your answers with the keys on page 68.
This page may be reproduced for classroom use.

17

Ghosts in the Night

PREPARATION

Key Words

next (nekst) coming right after this
My friend's house is down the <u>next</u> street.

night (nīt) the time of day after the sun goes down and
before the sun comes up
Wendy does not like being alone at <u>night</u>.

one (wun) more than none and less than two
<u>One</u> of my nephews is coming over to my house.
one in the morning; the first hour of a new day
*At <u>one</u> I looked up to see a ghost coming through my
door.*

three (thrē) one more than two
My <u>three</u> friends and I like to play ball.

when (hwen) at what time
Mom will help you <u>when</u> she gets home from work.

window (win´ dō) an opening in a wall that lets in light and air and is
usually covered with glass
Please close the <u>window</u> when night comes.

Ghosts in the Night

Necessary Words

bell   (bel)   a hollow cup that makes a sound when hit; in this story the bell tells what time it is by giving out one sound for each hour it is
> *I have to go home when the <u>bell</u> rings at two.*

crowd   (kroud)   a large number of people
> *I closed the door to stop the <u>crowd</u> from coming in.*

end   (end)   to stop
> *Our car ride had to <u>end</u> when my sister fell ill.*

hide   (hīd)   to put or keep where one will not be seen
> *When we were playing my friend wanted to <u>hide</u> in the house.*

ring   (ring)   to give out a clear sound as if from a bell
> *I run to the telephone when I hear it <u>ring</u>.*

suffer   (suf´ər)   to feel pain or sorrow
> *The poor <u>suffer</u> from the cold when it is winter.*

People, Places, and Things

Bed curtains   are screens of cloth that hang around all sides of a bed to make it like a small room. Bed curtains keep out the cold and give people privacy.

Ghosts in the Night

Marley tells Scrooge how he suffers now that he is dead.

Preview
1. Read the name of the story.
2. Look at the picture.
3. Read the sentence under the picture.
4. Read the first (   ) paragraphs of the story.
5. Then answer the following question.

You learned from your preview that Marley
_____a. likes being a ghost.
_____b. wants Scrooge to help him.
_____c. is not happy being a ghost.
_____d. is friends with the poor now.

Turn to the Comprehension Check on page 22 for the right answer.

Now read the story.
Read to find out who will come to help Scrooge.

Ghosts in the Night

"I suffer, Ebenezer," said Marley. "When I worked with you at the counting house, I walked when I wanted to walk. Now I can not stop walking! When I worked with you, I did not have to look at the poor. Now I can not stop seeing the poor! I see the poor suffer! I suffer with the poor! I can not help the poor now! Why did I not help?"

"I do not like seeing you like this, Marley!" said Scrooge. "I do not want to end up like you! Will you help me?"

"I can not help you," said Marley. "Three ghosts will come to help you."

"Three ghosts are coming here?" Scrooge said. "I do not want to see three ghosts! I will hide in my bed curtains!"

"Do you want to end up like me?" said Marley. "This night, when you hear the bell ring at one, a ghost will come to you. The next night, the next ghost will come when the bell rings at one."

"Why can not the three ghosts come in one night?" said Scrooge.

"You will see one ghost a night for three nights!" said Marley. "You do not want to suffer when you are dead like me. Come to the window. What do you see?" "I do not want to look!" said Scrooge.

"You will look," said Marley. He walked through the window.

"It is good to see Marley go!" said Scrooge. "I will close the window and end this ghost humbug!"

Scrooge looked through the window. "I do not believe what I see! Look at the crowd of ghosts walking through the night! I can not count the ghosts in this crowd. The ghosts are like Marley. The ghosts did not help the poor. Now the ghosts can not help! A ghost is stopping at my window! His counting house was next door to my counting house. Look at his chains! I can see he is suffering," Scrooge said. "Go away!"

Scrooge looked down. "What is the ghost down there doing? He is looking at a poor family. He wants to give something to the father. The ghost can not give money now. The father can not see the ghost wanting to help his poor family!"

"I do not like to see the ghosts suffer like this!" said Scrooge. He looked down through the window at the poor family. "I see the family. Why are the ghosts not there now?"

Scrooge closed the window. He walked to his door and looked at it. "Did I see ghosts or not? Did I see my friend Marley? I can not believe this is humbug, and I can not believe in ghosts!" Scrooge said. "I will hide in the bed curtains and see what comes when the bell rings at one!"

Ghosts in the Night

COMPREHENSION CHECK

Choose the best answer.

1. Now that he is dead, Marley can not stop
____a. making money.
____b. walking and seeing the poor.
____c. coming into peoples' houses.
____d. walking with the crowd of ghosts.

2. Scrooge wants Marley
____a. to help him make money.
____b. to show him how to help ghosts.
____c. to help him not end up like Marley.
____d. to get three ghosts to come see Scrooge.

3. When the three ghosts come, Scrooge plans to
____a. to hide.
____b. tell the ghosts to help Marley.
____c. jump out of the window.
____d. ask the ghosts to take off his chains.

4. Marley tells Scrooge the three ghosts will come
____a. all in one night.
____b. after Christmas.
____c. to the counting house.
____d. one each night.

5. Marley wants Scrooge to come to the window
____a. because Marley likes telling Scrooge what to do.
____b. to see the crowd of ghosts.
____c. because he wants Scrooge to come through the window.
____d. so Scrooge can hear the bell.

6. When Marley walks through the window, Scrooge
____a. is glad to see him go.
____b. worries Marley will fall.
____c. wants to go with him.
____d. tells Marley to come back.

7. The crowd of ghosts outside of Scrooge's window
____a. will walk away when Marley comes.
____b. want to come into Scrooge's house.
____c. are the ghosts of poor families.
____d. did not help the poor when the ghosts were still living.

8. After he stops seeing the crowd of ghosts Scrooge
____a. wishes Marley had told him more.
____b. believes ghosts are humbug.
____c. believes ghosts are real.
____d. hides to see what happens next.

9. Another name for this story could be
____a. "The Ghosts Come for Scrooge."
____b. "The Suffering Ghosts"
____c. "Marley Makes More Money."
____d. "Giving Money to the Poor."

10. This story is mainly about
____a. Scrooge seeing how some ghosts suffer.
____b. the ghosts walking through the night.
____c. Scrooge wanting to help the poor.
____d. three ghosts coming through Scrooge's door.

Check your answers with the keys on page 67.

Ghosts in the Night

VOCABULARY CHECK

next	night	one	three	when	window

I. Sentences to Finish
Fill in the blank in each sentence with the correct key word from the box above.

1. My home is _____ houses down from my Grandmother's.

2. I looked through the _____ to see Daddy coming home.

3. Do not play _____ to the car!

4. Sharon jumped _____ the ghost walked through the door.

5. There is _____ dog that barks at me!

6. Father said, "You have to stop playing and come in for the _____."

II. Crossword Puzzle
Use the words from the box above to fill in the puzzle. Use the sentences below to help you choose the right answers.

Across

1. After the sun goes down it is _____ .

3. If the ball hits the _____ it will break.

5. My family will come to my house

_____ Christmas.

Down

2. I have to go in _____ my mother calls me.

4. You may give _____ toy to your friend.

6. My _____ friends are coming with me.

Check your answers with the keys on page 69.
This page may be reproduced for classroom use.

The Ghost of Christmas Past

PREPARATION

Key Words

am	(am)	a form of "to be" used with the pronoun "I" *I am going to hide my money. I am happy that you came.*
boy	(boi)	a male child *Daniel asked the boy to play with us.*
girl	(gėrl)	a female child *Mother likes to tell us what she was like as a girl.*
light	(līt)	brightness given off that lets one see *The sun's light helps flowers grow.*
man	(man)	a grown-up male *Daddy said, "You will grow up to be a tall man like me.* the human race: men, women and children *Man has always wondered what happens to us after we are dead.*
school	(skül)	a place for teaching and learning *When Dickens was a boy, he lived away from home at his school.*

The Ghost of Christmas Past

Necessary Words

change   (chānj)   to become different
> *Your life will <u>change</u> after you learn to read.*

dance   (dans)   to move with rhythm, usually to music
> *Joan likes to watch Mother and Father <u>dance</u>.*

heart   (härt)   the part of the body that pumps blood; often the heart is said to be the place that holds one's emotions
> *Edith knew Jeff had a big <u>heart</u> when she saw him give money to a homeless man.*

remember   (ri mem´ bə r)   to think about something that happened to you
> *Do you <u>remember</u> the first time you flew in an airplane?*

touch   (tuch)   to give a soft tap
> Would you want to <u>touch</u> a ghost?

wrong   (rông)   not right
> *"Something is <u>wrong</u> with my car. It will not start!" said Bill.*

People, Places, and Things

Fan   was Scrooge's little sister and Fred's mother.

Fezziwig   was the owner of the first place where Scrooge worked.

The Ghost of Christmas Past   shows Scrooge what his Christmases were like when he was young. The Ghost seems to keep changing, just as it is sometimes hard to remember the past clearly.

The Ghost of Christmas Past

A Ghost who gives off light comes to Scrooge.

Preview   1. Read the name of the story.
2. Look at the picture.
3. Read the sentence under the picture.
4. Read the first (   ) paragraphs of the story.
5. Then answer the following question.

You learned from your preview that the Ghost
____a.   is Marley's friend.
____b.   has come when the bells ring at two.
____c.   came through Scrooge's door.
____d.   has a bright light coming from him.

Turn to the Comprehension Check on page 28 for the right answer.

Now read the story.
Read to find out what the Ghost of Christmas Past shows Scrooge.

The Ghost of Christmas Past

"Something is wrong with the bells! The bells are ringing and ringing!" Scrooge said. "Now what is going on? The bells have stopped. Now the bells are ringing in one! What is this light I see?"

The Ghost looked like a little boy. "I believe light makes up this boy," said Scrooge. "The light is making the Ghost change. The ghost was a boy. Now the ghost is a man. Now I see the light, and not the ghost! What are you?"

"I am the Ghost of Christmas Past."

"You are a little ghost," Scrooge said, for now the light was a little man. "I do not like the light. Can you hide it?"

"You do not want to look at me," said the Ghost of Christmas Past. "I can hide it a little. Come through the window."

"The ghostly dead can walk through a window. Man can not!" Scrooge said.

"I will touch you here," said the Ghost. He touched Scrooge's heart. "Now you may come."

"It was night at my house," said Scrooge. "Now it is light! I remember this! We are coming to my school. I was here when I was a boy. See the crowd of boys coming? The boys go to school with me. A good Christmas to you, my friends!"

"The boys can not see you, Scrooge," said the Ghost. "The boys are walking home for Christmas. One boy is here alone."

"There I am in the school," said Scrooge. "I was alone this Christmas, and the next one, and the next..."

"A little girl changed Christmas for you," said the Ghost.

Scrooge looked up. The boy was bigger now. "Here comes Fan!" Scrooge said.

"I have come for you, Ebenezer!" said the little girl. "You are to come home for good. Father is a changed man! He sees it now; he was wrong to make you go away!"

"I wanted to dance when Fan said I was to come home," Scrooge said to the Ghost. "It makes me want to dance now! It is good to see Fan!"

"The girl did have a big heart," said the Ghost. "Fan is dead now."

"Yes. She was the mother of my nephew Fred." Scrooge remembered when Fred stopped at the counting house on Christmas Eve. "I was not good to Fred."

Now it was night. Scrooge walked with the Ghost.

"I remember this door. I worked here for Fezziwig! Look, there I am!" Ebenezer, now a man, walked through the door. "Come look!" Scrooge said to the Ghost. "My friends and I danced through the night on this Christmas Eve! Fezziwig was a good man. Working for Fezziwig was like having a family."

Scrooge looked at the Ghost. He was not hiding his light now.

"What is wrong?" said the Ghost.

"I was not good to Bob Cratchit," said Scrooge. "I will change!"

The Ghost of Christmas Past

COMPREHENSION CHECK

Choose the best answer.

1. Scrooge thinks something is wrong with the bells because
____a. the bells are ringing and ringing.
____b. he can not hear the bells.
____c. he knows the bells are broken.
____d. light is coming from the bells.

2. When Scrooge looks at the Ghost
____a. the Ghost hides.
____b. Scrooge wants to run.
____c. the Ghost seems to change how he looks.
____d. Scrooge remembers Marley.

3. Scrooge wants the Ghost to
____a. get out of his house.
____b. hide his light.
____c. show Scrooge his old friends.
____d. use his light to walk through the night.

4. Scrooge does not like the Ghost's light because Scrooge
____a. does not want to remember what his past was like.
____b. likes the night.
____c. can not see the Ghost with so much light.
____d. does not want to be seen with a ghost.

5. As a boy, Scrooge passed many Christmases
____a. wanting to dance.
____b. having fun with his friends.
____c. visiting with his sister Fan
____d. alone at school.

6. Fan comes to Ebenezer's school
____a. to help carry his things.
____b. to ask his friends not to go without him.
____c. to bring him home for good.
____d. so that she can learn too.

7. When Scrooge worked for Fezziwig
____a. Ebenezer and Fan danced on Christmas Eve.
____b. Fezziwig was good to Ebenezer and his friends.
____c. Ebenezer was a boy.
____d. Ebenezer was in school.

8. Scrooge remembers that he was not good to
____a. Fan and his father.
____b. Marley and Bob Cratchit.
____c. Fred and Bob Cratchit.
____d. Fred and Fan.

9. Another name for this story could be
____a. "When Scrooge was Young."
____b. "Alone at School."
____c. "Dancing with Fezziwig."
____d. "Fan and Ebenezer."

10. This story is mainly about
____a. the Ghost changing how he looks.
____b. Scrooge remembering when he was a boy and young man.
____c. Scrooge being sent from his family.
____d. how the Ghost makes them jump from Christmas to Christmas.

Check your answers with the keys on page 67.

This page may be reproduced for classroom use.

The Ghost of Christmas Past

VOCABULARY CHECK

am	boy	girl	light	man	school

I. Sentences to Finish
Fill in the blank in each sentence with the correct key word from the box above.

1. Tell the _____ in the green dress that she is a fast runner!

2. Now that I go to _____ I can read!

3. I _____ going to borrow my friend's toy.

4. Mother said, "John, you are a good little _____."

5. A _____ will help you see at night.

6. My little brother said, "When I grow up to be a _____, I will have three cars!"

II. Fill in the Blanks with Definitions
In the blank space in each sentence, write the correct key word that means the same as the words under the line.

1. Charlotte walks to _____ with her friends in the morning.
   a place to learn

2. The _____ is helping her mother.
   female child

3. Shine the _____ over here so that I can see the door.
   brightness to see by

4. I _____ making cookies right now.
   be

5. The _____ standing over there is Jerry's father.
   grown-up male

6. The little _____ believes ghosts will run after him.
   male child

Check your answers with the keys on page 69.
This page may be reproduced for classroom use.

Love for Belle

PREPARATION

Key Words

be   (bē)   to exist or to happen
> *Be good to your friends. When will they be coming?*

cry   (krī)   to have tears come from one's eyes
> *I cry when I hear a sad story.*

her   (her)   the girl or woman who is being talked about
> *Max told her to come home now.*

              belonging to a girl or woman
> *Give Kathy her money now!*

laugh   (laf)   to make a sound that shows one is happy or thinks something is funny
> *You laugh when you hear a good joke.*

more   (môr)   a greater size or number
> *Please give me more!*

              greater in size or number
> *Todd wants more ice cream.*

              to a greater degree
> *I like the blue hat more than the red.*

woman   (wŭm´ə n)   a grown-up female
> *Your mother is a good woman.*

Love for Belle

Necessary Words

afraid (ə frād´) to be scared
The family was not <u>afraid</u> of ghosts before they moved into the house.

face (fās) the front of one's head; one's eyes, nose, and mouth
Rain ran down Arthur's <u>face</u> and off his chin.

love (luv) strong liking
Jacob's <u>love</u> of books grew from his reading.

to have strong liking for
Raymond will always <u>love</u> his mother.

marry (mar´ ē) to take as a husband or a wife
Yvonne will <u>marry</u> Tony when she is older.

push (push) to press against something
You must <u>push</u> the door to close it.

world (werld) all existing things and people; everything on the earth
The <u>world</u> would be better if people stopped fighting.

People, Places and Things

Belle is the woman Scrooge once loved. "Belle" means beautiful in French. Her name sounds like the word "bell."

31

Love for Belle

The Ghost shows Scrooge the woman he loved when he was young.

Preview   1. Read the name of the story.
2. Look at the picture.
3. Read the sentence under the picture.
4. Read the first (   ) paragraphs of the story.
5. Then answer the following question.

You learned from your preview that
____a.   Belle likes to laugh.
____b.   Ebenezer has said that he loves Belle.
____c.   Belle is a friend of Fan.
____d.   Ebenezer is still working for Fezziwig.

Turn to the Comprehension Check on page 34 for the right answer.

Now read the story.
Read to find out what man Belle will marry.

Love for Belle

"There is more for you to see," said the Ghost of Christmas Past.

"There I am with Belle!" said Scrooge. "I loved her when I was working for Fezziwig. Belle changed when I stopped working there."

"You liked to laugh when you worked for Fezziwig," said the Ghost. "You do not look like you want to laugh here. Look!"

Ebenezer was walking with a woman. "Do not cry, Belle!" Ebenezer said to her.

"You have said you love me," said Belle. "Now I see you love money more! Will money help you when I go, and you are alone?"

"Look at the world. The world runs down the poor," said Ebenezer. "Why is it wrong to want to make more and more money?"

"You are afraid of the world," said Belle. "You do not want to be touched by the world. You are afraid the world will make you suffer. You have changed!"

"I have changed when it comes to the world," said Ebenezer. "I have not changed when it comes to my love for you."

"I am not afraid of being poor," said Belle. "I am afraid of not being loved. I can not marry you, Ebenezer. I do not believe you want to marry a poor woman like me." Hiding her face, Belle walked away.

"I did not push you away!" said Ebenezer. "You wanted this!"

"Go with her!" Scrooge said to Ebenezer. "Make her stop crying! Marry her!"

"He can not hear you," the Ghost said. "Why did I not stop her? Belle was the one woman I have loved," said Scrooge. "I was afraid to remember my love for her."

"There is more to see," said the Ghost.

"Is this Belle's house?" said Scrooge. "Look at her playing with her crowd of boys and girls. Belle is a good mother. A man is walking through the door. Did this man marry my Belle? Is this his and her family?"

"Yes," said the Ghost.

"Coming home, I walked by the counting house," the man said to Belle. "You will not believe what Scrooge is up to!"

"Scrooge?" laughed Belle. "Was he counting his money?"

"Do you remember his friend Marley?" said the man. "He works with Scrooge at the counting house. One night something was wrong with Marley. He did not look good. Marley walked home. Scrooge did not want to stop working. He did not want to go see his friend. Now Marley is dead."

Scrooge was crying. "I want to go home!" he said to the Ghost. "Bah! I do not like this light you make!" Scrooge looked at the Ghost. The Ghost's face was changing. "You look like Belle...now Fezziwig...now my little Fan! I do not want to see more faces. I do not want to see more light. Go away!" Scrooge pushed down on the little ghost. He pushed away the light. "Good!" said Scrooge. "Now I am alone!"

33

Love for Belle

COMPREHENSION CHECK

Choose the best answer.

1. Ebenezer fell in love with Belle
____a. but was afraid to tell her.
____b. when they were laughing together.
____c. because she had money.
____d. while he was working for Fezziwig.

2. Ebenezer thinks the world
____a. will help him when he is down.
____b. is full of people he can make money from.
____c. is making Belle cry.
____d. will not help the poor.

3. Belle believes Ebenezer
____a. is wrong to think money will keep him safe from the world.
____b. thinks too much about how the world sees him.
____c. will always love her.
____d. is right about how the world is to the poor.

4. Belle does not marry Ebenezer because
____a. she does not like his family.
____b. he loves money more than her.
____c. she does not love him.
____d. he does not have the money to marry her.

5. When Scrooge sees Belle walk away, he
____a. remembers that he did not really want to marry her.
____b. wishes he had stopped her and married her.
____c. believes the Ghost is making him remember things wrong.
____d. believes the world wanted to end his love for Belle.

Preview Answer:
b.   Ebenezer has said that he loves Belle.

---

6. After Belle left Ebenezer, she
____a. was never happy.
____b. worked for a family with a lot of money.
____c. married a man and became a mother.
____d. wished she had married Scrooge.

7. The man who married Belle said that Scrooge
____a. did not stop working to see Marley before he died.
____b. was crying.
____c. was wrong not to marry Belle.
____d. wants to be alone on Christmas Eve.

8. Scrooge pushes the Ghost of Christmas Past when he
____a. hears the next ghost coming.
____b. sees the face of someone he did not like.
____c. wants the Ghost to show him another Christmas in his past.
____d. suffers too much from remembering the past.

9. Another name for the story could be
____a. "The Sad Life of Belle."
____b. "Good-by to the Ghost."
____c. "Remembering Belle."
____d. "Ending the Light."

10. The story is mainly about
____a. Scrooge not wanting to get married.
____b. how Belle found another love.
____c. the Ghost telling Scrooge he was wrong.
____d. what happened when Scrooge wanted money more than love.

Check your answers with the keys on page 67.

Love for Belle

VOCABULARY CHECK

be	cry	her	laugh	more	woman

I. Sentences to Finish
Fill in the blank in each sentence with the correct key word from the box above.

1. The _____ next door is a my mother's friend.

2. I will _____ here when you come home.

3. My friend is very funny. She makes me _____!

4. If you want help, I can do _____ work.

5. The little girl will _____ when she sees the toys are gone.

6. Margie wants _____ nephew to come over to the house.

II. Word Search Scramble
The keywords in the box above are hidden in the puzzle below. They may be written from left to right or up and down. As you find each word, put a circle around it. Unscramble the six letters that you have not circled to answer the question under the puzzle.

```
B   R   A   W   E
E   E   R   O   M
M   H   L   M   Y
H   G   U   A   L
C   R   Y   N   R
```

The name of the first ghost to visit Scrooge was ___ ___ ___ ___ ___ ___.

Check your answers with the keys on page 70.
This page may be reproduced for classroom use.

The Ghost of Christmas Present

PREPARATION

Key Words

over	(ō vər)	above a place *Janice hit the ball <u>over</u> my head.* across a space *When can you come <u>over</u> to my house?*
many	(men´ ē)	being made up of a large number *The dog was so strong he broke <u>many</u> chains.*
never	(ne´ vər)	not ever; not in any way *Jane <u>never</u> says anything bad about a friend.*
room	(rüm)	a part of a house that has its own walls *The door to my <u>room</u> keeps closing by itself!*
street	(strēt)	a smoothed down way that a town or a city builds that people use to get to places *A man is walking his dog down our <u>street</u>.*
than	(Ŧhan)	when compared to *Marsha can jump higher <u>than</u> I can.*

The Ghost of Christmas Present

Necessary Words

brothers (bruŦH´ə rz) boys or men who have the same mother and father
My little sister is always asking our brothers to help her.

cook (ku̇k) to use heat to make food ready to eat
When you cook over a fire, do not burn your hands!

food (füd) what can be eaten to help a living being live
Good food helps you grow strong.

sprinkle (spring´ kə l) to drop little bits of something
Mom showed me how to sprinkle sugar over the cake.

seen (sēn) a past tense of "to see"
Have you seen many houses this big?

torch (tôrch) a light that is carried by its handle
The rain put out the fire in our torch.

People, Places, and Things

A Baker's Shop had ovens, but most poor people did not. The poor could not cook some kinds of foods in their fireplaces. On Christmas, baker's shops were not allowed to sell their breads and cakes. But the shops could use the ovens to cook the food of the poor. The poor gave the shops a little money for this help.

Eighteen Hundred is about how many brothers the Ghost has. His brothers are the Christmases that have come before him. When the Ghost talks about having more than eighteen hundred brothers, he is saying more than 1800 Christmases have come before him. Dickens wrote "A Christmas Carol" in the year 1843.

The Ghost of Christmas Present shows Scrooge the Christmas that is happening at this time in Scrooge's life.

The Ghost of Christmas Past

Scrooge sees a big ghost in the next room.

Preview   1. Read the name of the story.
　　　　　　2. Look at the picture.
　　　　　　3. Read the sentence under the picture.
　　　　　　4. Read the first (　) paragraphs of the story.
　　　　　　5. Then answer the following question.

You learned from your preview that Scrooge
____a. is going to push the next ghost away.
____b. is afraid the Ghost of Christmas Past will come back.
____c.   thinks the next ghost will not come.
____d. wants to know what the next ghost will look like.

Turn to the Comprehension Check on page 40 for the right answer.

Now read the story.
Read to find out where the next ghost takes Scrooge.

The Ghost of Christmas Present

"It is good to be alone," Scrooge said. "I did not like the Ghost of Christmas Past. He can not make me suffer now." Scrooge walked to his room. "Marley said I was to see one ghost a night. I want this night to end! I want to get on to the next night and the next ghost!

"What am I hearing now? The bells are ringing," Scrooge said. "The bells are wrong. It can not be one! The Ghost of Christmas Past was here at one. Is the next ghost coming now? I will not hide in the bed curtains. I want to see this next ghost when he comes. What will he look like?

"I see a ghostly red light," Scrooge said. He walked over to the door of his room. A big ghost was in the next room! Afraid, Scrooge looked away.

"I am the Ghost of Christmas Present," said the Ghost. "Look at me!"

Scrooge looked up. The ghost's big red face looked friendly. The ghost's torch was giving a red light to the room. Scrooge liked this ghost more than the Ghost of Christmas Past.

"You have never seen the like of me!" said the Ghost.

"Never!" said Scrooge.

"You have never walked with my brothers?" said the Ghost.

"I do not believe I have," said Scrooge. "Do you have many brothers?"

"I have more than eighteen hundred!" said the Ghost.

"You have a big family to get food for," said Scrooge.

"Come with me," said the Ghost.

"It is Christmas!" Scrooge laughed. He liked walking down the street with this Ghost. "Look through the windows! The boys and girls are playing with toys. The mother is in the next room. What food will the mother cook for Christmas? Here comes the father with more food and more toys to give!"

Scrooge looked down the street. "There are many poor families coming up this street," Scrooge said.

The poor did not see the Ghost and Scrooge. "The poor are going to the baker's shop," said the Ghost. "He will cook the little food the poor have for Christmas." The Ghost walked over to the families. He touched his torch to sprinkle something over the food. When the torch sprinkled over the food, the families laughed.

"I did not see the food change when you sprinkled it," said Scrooge.

"Now the food is touched by Christmas," said the Ghost. "Christmas touches food given with a good heart. It touches the food of the poor the most."

"Why?" said Scrooge.

"Christmas helps the poor the most," said the Ghost.

Scrooge and the Ghost walked down many streets. The Ghost stopped at a poor little house. "Here we are," said the Ghost.

"Why are we stopping here?" Scrooge looked up at the Ghost. "I have never seen this house."

"You have never come here?" asked the Ghost. "This is Bob Cratchit's house!"

The Ghost of Christmas Present

COMPREHENSION CHECK

Choose the best answer.

1. Scrooge thinks the bells are wrong because
____a. the bells are saying it is one for the second time in one night.
____b. he believes Marley will come back now.
____c. night is almost over.
____d. the next ghost will come at two.

2. Scrooge can tell the next ghost has come when
____a. he hears laughing.
____b. the bed curtains fall down.
____c. he sees a ghostly red light.
____d. the Ghost tells him to look at him.

3. Scrooge thinks the Ghost of Christmas Present
____a. will stop the next ghost from coming.
____b. is big and friendly.
____c. may not be the ghost Scrooge is looking for.
____d. may do something bad to his house.

4. When the Ghost asks if Scrooge has walked with his brothers, he wants to know if Scrooge
____a. has enjoyed other Christmases in his past.
____b. likes to walk at night.
____c. can tell the Ghost where to find food.
____d. has brothers of his own.

5. Scrooge looks through windows to see
____a. a family who borrowed money from his counting house.
____b. Scrooge passing Christmas alone.
____c. how a family with money passes Christmas.
____d. how he danced all night at Fezziwig's.

6. The poor families are going to the baker's shop
____a. to see when the shop opens.
____b. to have their food cooked.
____c. to get cookies and cakes for Christmas.
____d. to get warm in the shop.

7. The Ghost of Christmas Present sprinkles his torch over
____a. Scrooge to make him see the poor.
____b. the food to help make the poor happy.
____c. the baker's shop to thank him.
____d. the poor to show them Christmas.

8. The Ghost of Christmas Present stops Scrooge
____a. at the counting house.
____b. from remembering Belle.
____c. in front of Bob Cratchit's house.
____d. from looking in the windows of houses.

9. Another name for this story could be
____a. "Christmas on the Streets."
____b. "Never Let a Ghost In!"
____c. "A Sad Christmas."
____d. "A Big Ghost with a Big Heart."

10. This story is mainly about
____a. families with money and their Christmas.
____b. Scrooge should not be afraid of ghosts.
____c. the Ghost helps poor people.
____d. Scrooge likes Christmas when he is with this ghost.

Check your answers with the keys on page 67.

The Ghost of Christmas Present

VOCABULARY CHECK

over	many	never	room	street	than

I. Sentences to Finish
Fill in the blank in each sentence with the correct key word from the box above.

1. Three is more _____ one.

2. I see a light coming through the door of Donna's _____.

3. The airplane is flying _____ the houses.

4. Barbara has _____ friends to help her when she is down.

5. The car was going too fast down our _____.

6. Stephen _____ married the woman he loved.

II. Story Fill-in
Fill in the blanks in the following story using the key words above. Each key word is used only once.

When I saw our new house I was a little afraid. It was night. We got out of our car and looked up at the house. "You will like your (1)_____ here," Mom said.

I looked up. "I see a ghost in the window!" I said. "I am (2)_____ going into this house!"

"You do not see a ghost. Come in and look," said Mom. "I believe you will like this house more (3)_____ our last home."

The next day the house did not make me afraid. There are (4)_____ boys and girls living on this (5)_____. When they came (6)_____ to my house, I made new friends!

Check your answers with the keys on page 70.
This page may be reproduced for classroom use.

Christmas at the Cratchits' House

PREPARATION

Key Words

as	(az)	a word used to compare things that are alike *This painting is just <u>as</u> good as the other one.* during the time of *<u>As</u> we were coming through the door we heard the telephone.*
every	(ev′ rē)	each one in a group *You have to pick up <u>every</u> toy in this room!*
from	(frum)	out of *The light <u>from</u> the sun is very bright.*
live	(liv)	to have life; to exist *Some people say you will <u>live</u> longer the more you laugh.*
people	(pē′ p l)	men, women, girls and boys *My brothers are friends with many <u>people</u>.*
us	(us)	the person who is speaking along with others *Will you help <u>us</u> do our work? Which one of us will go?*

Christmas at the Cratchits' House

Necessary Words

bless (bles) to ask for God's help or kindness
When Grandmom saw my brother for the first time she said, "Bless this baby."

crutch (kruch) a stick that fits under one's arm on one end and reaches the ground with the other
After my father hurt his foot he had to use a crutch to walk.

goose (güs) a large bird which has a long neck
We saw a goose swimming in the lake.

held (held) did not let go of; the past tense of "to hold'
I held the bag in one hand as I opened the door.

song (song) words that one sings
Peter is always happy to hear that song.

wife (wīf) a woman who is married
"I am going to marry Sarah," Tyler said. "I want her to be my wife."

People, Places and Things

Christ was born over 2,000 years ago. We tell what year it is by counting the years from his birth. Christ did not believe that people with a lot of money were any better than poor people.

Martha is Bob's daughter who is already working. In Charles Dickens' time, some children as young as 5 years old already had jobs.

Pudding in Dickens' time was usually made of beef fat, flour, eggs, raisins, and some sugar. The pudding was put in a cloth bag and boiled over a fire for many hours.

To Toast someone is to wish good things will happen to him. After someone is toasted, everyone usually has a sip of a drink.

Christmas at the Cratchits' House

Scrooge and the Ghost look on as the family gets their food ready.

Preview
1. Read the name of the story.
2. Look at the picture.
3. Read the sentence under the picture.
4. Read the first (   ) paragraphs of the story.
5. Then answer the following question.

You learned from your preview that Bob Cratchit's house
____a. is full of good food.
____b. has a lot of people in it.
____c. is next to the baker's shop.
____d. is too little for the Ghost to fit in.

Turn to the Comprehension Check on page 46 for the right answer.

Now read the story.
Read to find out who Scrooge sees at the Cratchits' house.

Christmas at the Cratchits' House

"A sprinkling from my torch will bless this home," said the Ghost.

Scrooge held on to the ghost as he walked through the door. "There are many people, and now one big ghost, in this little house," said Scrooge.

Bob's wife was cooking. Her girls and boys played in the room. "When will Martha get home from work?" said the mother.

"Martha is here," said a girl. The girl danced as Martha walked through the door. "Martha! The goose is cooking at the baker's shop! You have never seen a goose as big as this one!"

Martha laughed. "Have you seen every goose in the world?"

"You have come!" the mother said to Martha.

"I worked through the night," said Martha.

"Here come Father and Tiny Tim!" said the boys. "Hide, Martha, hide!" The boys pushed Martha into the next room. "Do not laugh in there!" the boys said.

Bob walked through the door. He held a little boy. The little boy held a crutch.

"The boy can not walk?" Scrooge said to the Ghost. "He looks like he may not live!"

Bob looked at the faces in the room. "Why is Martha not here?"

"Martha is not coming," said his wife.

"Not coming for Christmas?" said Bob.

Running from the next room, Martha touched her father's face. The family laughed.

"Come hear the pudding, Tim! It makes a song as it cooks!" The boys and girls helped Tim through the door.

Bob was alone with his wife. "Tim said something to me on the walk home. Tim said, 'It is good for people to see me on Christmas. Seeing me helps people remember the poor people Christ helped.'"

Two boys pushed through the door. "We will get the goose from the baker's shop."

"I will get the pudding when you come with the goose," said Bob's wife.

When the food was there, Scrooge looked at the goose. "This is little food for many people," he said to the Ghost.

"Bless us on this Christmas!" Bob said to his family.

"Bless us every one!" said Tiny Tim.

Scrooge looked at Tim's crutch. "Will Tiny Tim live?"

"When my next brother comes," said the Ghost, "Tim will not be here."

"Can this be changed?" said Scrooge.

"Do you remember what you said to the gentleman at the counting house on Christmas Eve?" said the Ghost.

"I said I wanted the poor to go away," said Scrooge. "I did not want to have to look at the poor. I was wrong. I want Tim to live!"

"We will toast Ebenezer Scrooge," said Bob.

"I will not toast Scrooge!" said his wife. "Scrooge's heart is closed to family and friends!"

Scrooge jumped. "It is good Bob's wife can not see us," said the Ghost.

"It is Christmas!" said Bob.

"I love you, Bob," said his wife. "I will toast Scrooge for you!"

"I want to hear a song from Tim!" said Martha.

"We will go now," the Ghost said to Scrooge.

Christmas at the Cratchits' House

COMPREHENSION CHECK

Choose the best answer.

1. Mrs. Cratchit wants to know when Martha will
____a. get home from work.
____b. go to the baker's shop.
____c. play with the other girls and boys.
____d. bring Bob and Tiny Tim home.

2. The girl tells Martha the goose is big because she
____a. is so happy about the goose that it looks very big to her.
____b. wants to trick Martha.
____c. hopes the baker's shop will give them a bigger goose.
____d. is too little to know what the word "big" means.

3. Martha hides from her father so that
____a. he will not be mad that she worked all night.
____b. she can hear what he says about her.
____c. she can surprise him and make him laugh.
____d. he will not take the money she worked for.

4. When he sees Tiny Tim, Scrooge
____a. says he did not know Bob was so strong to carry the boy.
____b. tries to tell Bob and Tim where Martha is hiding.
____c. learns that Tim can not walk.
____d. tells the Ghost that Tim will not live.

5. The boys and girls want Tiny Tim
____a. to come play with them.
____b. to hear the sound the pudding makes as it cooks.
____c. to find Martha for them.
____d. to help get the goose from the baker's shop.

6. Tiny Tim says it's good for people to see him because they will
____a. want to help him.
____b. stop looking away when they see the poor.
____c. be happy that they have money.
____d. remember the ways Christ helped the poor.

7. Scrooge wants Tiny Tim to live because
____a. he does not want Bob to be sad.
____b. his heart has been touched by Tiny Tim.
____c. he wants Tim to help at the counting house.
____d. he thinks Tim would like Scrooge if he met him.

8. Bob Cratchit wants his wife to toast Scrooge because
____a. he wants Scrooge to live so Bob has work.
____b. Scrooge will find out if Bob does not toast him.
____c. he wants his wife to be kinder to people.
____d. he is thankful to Scrooge even if he pays him very little.

9. Another name for this story could be
____a. "The Song of the Pudding."
____b. "Family Cooking."
____c. "Martha Misses Christmas."
____d. "A House Full of Love."

10. This story is mainly about Scrooge
____a. seeing the way Bob's family lives.
____b. not liking how Bob spends his money.
____c. learning that the Cratchits are one of many poor families.
____d. seeing he would be happy as a poor man.

Check your answers with the keys on page 67.

Christmas at the Cratchits' House

VOCABULARY CHECK

as	every	from	live	people	us

I. Sentences to Finish
Fill in the blank in each sentence with the correct key word from the box above.

1. Colby got on the airplane with _____.

2. When my dog and I go for a walk we go down _____ street.

3. Paula would not be afraid to _____ alone.

4. Linda was laughing _____ she danced.

5. May I borrow money _____ you?

6. There was a crowd of _____ on the street.

II Cryptogram
Fill the sentences below with the keywords in the box above. One letter fits in each space. Using the numbers below each space, answer the question.

1 The two brothers are __ __ __ __ the same family.
          2   8   6   3

2. Mom and I like to talk __ __ we cook lunch.
                          9   1

3. __ __ __ __ __ bird in the garden is afraid of my cat.
   4   5   4   8   12

4. Most __ __ __ __ __ __ like to eat pudding.
        10 4   6   10 11 4

5. Will you give __ __ a ride to the store?
                 13 1

6. Where do you want to __ __ __ __ when you grow up?
                         11 7   5   4

Question: What does Mrs. Cratchit want at the beginning of the story?

Answer: __H__   W__NT__   __ __ __TH__   T__
      1   4   9   1   3   9   8   9   6

  C__ __ __   H__ __ __.
  6   3   4   6   3   4

Check your answers with the keys on page 71.
This page may be reproduced for classroom use.

47

A Happy Night Ends

PREPARATION

Key Words

ask   (ask)   to try to find out with words
Doug is going to <u>ask</u> Millie to marry him.

does   (duz)   to do
<u>Does</u> that hat keep you warm?
He <u>does</u> not want to go with us.

happy   (hap´ ē)   glad, pleased, cheerful
Maurice has a good life but he is never <u>happy</u>.

old   (ōld)   having lived for a long time
The <u>old</u> woman grew wise from all she had seen in her life.

they   (ŦHā)   the people, animals, and things talked about
Put the kittens in the box before <u>they</u> run away.

your/yours (yu̇r)   1. owned by you, or having to do with you
Look out of <u>your</u> window to see if it is snowing.
            (yu̇rz)   2. the ones that belong to you
I can not tell my shoes from <u>yours</u>.

A Happy Night Ends

Necessary Words

beware	(bi wâr´)	to be careful of what might hurt you
		Beware of the dog! He may bite you!
float	(flōt)	to be held up by air or water
		We watched the balloons float up into the clouds.
himself	(him self´)	his own person
		Rob wants the candy for himself.
hurt	(hėrt)	to do damage or to cause pain
		Do not close the car window now or you will hurt your hand.
robe	(rōb)	a kind of loose clothing that has sleeves and that covers most of one's body
		The magician hid a rabbit in his robe.
should	(shůd)	ought to
		Wade should help his little brothers clean the room.

People, Places, and Things

Ignorance   is the name of the boy who is with the Ghost of Christmas Present. He is all the people who are not allowed to go to school. Dickens believed that education was an important way to help poor people.

Want   is the name of the girl that comes with Ignorance. She is all the poor people who do not have food, clothing, or a place to live.

A Happy Night Ends

The people below Scrooge and the Ghost are happy because it is Christmas.

Preview
1. Read the name of the story.
2. Look at the picture.
3. Read the sentence under the picture.
4. Read the first (   ) paragraphs of the story.
5. Then answer the following question.

You learned from your preview that the Ghost of Christmas Present
_____a. is saying good-by to Scrooge.
_____b. will drop Scrooge if he does not change.
_____c. is showing Scrooge the people of the world.
_____d. wants Scrooge to sing with him.

Turn to the Comprehension Check on page 52 for the right answer.

Now read the story.
Read to find out where Scrooge and the Ghost visit.

A Happy Night Ends

"I do not like to float over the world like this!" Scrooge said as he held on to the Ghost's robe.

"Look down!" said the Ghost. "See the many people of the world!"

Scrooge looked down through the night. "There are more than I can count."

"The people of the world love Christmas," said the Ghost. "Do you hear the Christmas songs?"

"What I hear," said Scrooge, "is my nephew laughing."

The night changed, and Scrooge was at Fred's house. His nephew was laughing. His many friends laughed with Fred.

"You have to believe me," laughed Fred. "Old Scrooge said Christmas is a humbug!"

"I do not like Scrooge," said his wife.

"He does not hurt us," said Fred. "He hurts himself when he pushes us away. Money will never make Scrooge happy."

"I am happy he is not here!" said Fred's wife.

"I will ask Scrooge to come next Christmas," said Fred. "I will not give up on the old man."

Scrooge and the Ghost looked on as the friends played songs. "I remember this song from when I was a boy," Scrooge said. "It makes me happy to hear it now!"

Topper was Fred's funny friend. He held on to a woman. "You are my love," Topper said. "Am I yours?" The woman laughed and pushed him away.

"This woman should beware of Topper!" Scrooge laughed. "He wants to marry her. He will work more on making her laugh than on making her money!"

"We have to go," said the Ghost.

"I liked seeing Fred and his friends," Scrooge said as they walked from the house. "I should go to my nephew's house when he can see me!"

Scrooge stopped in the street. "I hear the bells ringing!" Scrooge looked up at the Ghost. "Why does your face look old now?" Scrooge asked.

"This is the one night I live," said the Ghost.

"I see something hiding in your robe," Scrooge said.

A boy and a girl pushed through the robe. They looked up at Scrooge as they held on to the Ghost. "I can see they have suffered," Scrooge said to himself. "I want to see something good in this boy and girl. I can not! Something makes me afraid they will hurt me!"

"Are they yours?" Scrooge asked.

"They are Man's," said the Ghost. "This Christmas, they have held on to me, asking for help. The boy is Ignorance. The girl is Want. Beware of the girl. Beware of the boy more. The suffering you see on his face will hurt Man."

"People should help!" said Scrooge. "Why do they not help!"

"Are there no prisons?" asked the Ghost. "Are there no workhouses?"

"I should have given money for the poor to the gentleman on Christmas Eve," Scrooge said to himself. When he looked up, Scrooge was alone. "I have seen two ghosts. Marley said there will be one more." He looked down the street. A ghost was floating over to Scrooge.

A Happy Night Ends

COMPREHENSION CHECK

Preview Answer:
c. is showing Scrooge the people of the world.

Choose the best answer.

1. The Ghost wants Scrooge to see that many people of the world
   ____a. sing in the night.
   ____b. love Christmas.
   ____c. live near Fred's house.
   ____d. see Scrooge floating over them.

2. When Scrooge and the Ghost come to Fred's house
   ____a. Fred and his wife are alone.
   ____b. the Ghost says Scrooge must come to Fred's next Christmas.
   ____c. Fred's wife is afraid Scrooge will come.
   ____d. Fred is laughing about Scrooge calling Christmas "a humbug."

3. Fred laughs about Scrooge but he
   ____a. loves Scrooge even as he laughs at his ideas.
   ____b. thinks his wife is right about Scrooge.
   ____c. is hurt Scrooge did not come for Christmas.
   ____d. will saying anything to get a good laugh.

4. Fred says Scrooge hurts himself by
   ____a. pushing away the people who love him.
   ____b. saving his money when he should enjoy it.
   ____c. walking around all night with a ghost.
   ____d. working at the counting house.

5. Fred's friend Topper wants
   ____a. to make more people laugh than Fred does.
   ____b. to make the woman he loves marry him.
   ____c. find out how much money the woman has.
   ____d. to make Fred's wife like Scrooge.

6. When Scrooge first hears the bells ringing he sees
   ____a. the friends coming out of Fred's house.
   ____b. the next ghost coming.
   ____c. something hiding in the Ghost's robe.
   ____d. that the Ghost's face now looks old.

7. The boy and girl holding on to the Ghost's robe should be helped by
   ____a. the Ghost of Christmas Present.
   ____b. the next ghost to come.
   ____c. Scrooge and other people who are able to help.
   ____d. Bob Cratchit and his family.

8. When the Ghost asks if there are no prisons and workhouses,
   ____a. the boy and girl become afraid they will be sent away.
   ____b. Scrooge pushes him away.
   ____c. he is saying the same thing Scrooge said at the counting house.
   ____d. he wants to make Scrooge laugh.

9. Another name for this story could be
   ____a. "At Fred's House."
   ____b. "Topper Gets a Wife."
   ____c. "Ignorance and Want."
   ____d. "The Next Ghost Comes."

10. This story is mainly about
   ____a. Scrooge wanting to come to Fred's house next Christmas.
   ____b. Christmas is a happy time when people should help each other.
   ____c. the next ghost coming to see Scrooge.
   ____d. the Ghost wanting Scrooge to take away the boy and girl.

Check your answers with the keys on page 67.

A Happy Night Ends

VOCABULARY CHECK

ask	does	happy	old	they	your

I. Sentences to Finish
Fill in the blank in each sentence with the correct key word from the box above.

1. Alton and Faith said that _____ will not be coming.

2. I will be _____ when my friend comes over.

3. Please _____ the man when the play will end.

4. When _____ cat jumped on my dog, he ran away!

5. Many people do not hear as well when they grow _____.

6. Kristen _____ not like the new red car.

II. Words Which Do Not Belong
Use the blank space to write the word that does not belong.

1. Which word does <u>not</u> belong with **your**? _____
   a. my   b. his   c. she

2. Which word does <u>not</u> belong with **ask**? _____
   a. this   b. why   c. what

3. Which word does <u>not</u> belong with **happy**? _____
   a. laughing b. glad   c. never

4. Which word does <u>not</u> belong with **they**? _____
   a. over   b. we   c. she

5. Which word does <u>not</u> belong with **old**? _____
   a. elderly b. kitten c. aged

6. Which word does <u>not</u> belong with **does**? _____
   a. are   b. light   d. be

Check your answers with the keys on page 71.
This page may be reproduced for classroom use.

The Ghost of Christmas Yet to Come

PREPARATION

Key Words

bed	(bed)	a place to sleep or to rest *I went to sleep as soon as I got into my <u>bed</u>.*
black	(blak)	a very dark color *The words in this book are printed with <u>black</u> ink.*
take	(tāk)	to get hold of *Do not <u>take</u> money that is not yours.*
		to use *It will <u>take</u> work to fix the car.*
things	(thingz)	what belongs to someone *Father said, "Please do not leave your <u>things</u> in front of the door."*
time	(tīm)	the days that there have been and will be *Man has changed his world over <u>time</u>.*
		part of time *We do not have <u>time</u> to stop at the school.*
who	(hü)	which person or people *<u>Who</u> was at the party?*
		a word used to refer back to a person or people in the sentence *I have many friends <u>who</u> make me laugh.*

The Ghost of Christmas Yet to Come

Necessary Words

bury   (ber´ ē)   to put something no longer alive (dead) into the ground
> *When my dog died, Mom said we could <u>bury</u> him in the flower garden.*

care   (ker)   to feel interest or concern
> *Russ does not <u>care</u> about how he looks.*

fell   (fel)   to have dropped or come down
> *The red leaves <u>fell</u> from the tree.*

pointed   (poin´ tid)   to have shown the way by holding out one's finger
> *A man <u>pointed</u> the way to your house.*

sheet   (shēt)   a wide piece of cloth used on a bed
> *When my little brother wants to dress up like a ghost, he pulls the <u>sheet</u> off my bed.*

shirt   (shėrt)   a piece of clothing that covers a person's top half
> *My blue <u>shirt</u> has holes in the sleeves.*

People, Places, and Things

A charwoman   is a woman who is paid to help clean one's house.

The Ghost of Christmas Yet To Come   will show Scrooge what will happen in the time to come.

A laundress   is a woman who is paid to wash clothes and bedding.

A rag-and-bone man   takes old things that people do not want and sells them. He collects rags to be made into new clothing or paper. He collects bones to be made into glue.

An undertaker's man   helps the undertaker get a body ready to be buried. In Dickens' time, a body would often stay in the family home until it was time to be buried.

The Ghost of Christmas Yet to Come

Scrooge is very afraid of this ghost. He can not see his face!

Preview   1. Read the name of the story.
2. Look at the picture.
3. Read the sentence under the picture.
4. Read the first (   ) paragraphs of the story.
5. Then answer the following question.

You learned from your preview that the Ghost of Christmas Yet to Come
    ____a. will help Scrooge remember all the good he has done.
    ____b. looks just like the Ghost of Christmas Present.
    ____c.   makes Scrooge afraid.
    ____d. is taking Scrooge to Fred's house.

Turn to the Comprehension Check on page 58 for the right answer.

Now read the story.
Read to find out what the Ghost shows Scrooge.

The Ghost of Christmas Yet to Come

The Ghost's robe was as black as the night. "Your robe hides your face," said Scrooge. "Are you the Ghost of Christmas Yet to Come? I am afraid of you! Will you take me to see what will come in time?"

The black robe touched Scrooge's face. The Ghost pointed at two people walking through the night. "They work down the street from my counting house," Scrooge said.

"I hear he is dead," said one man.

"What do I care?" said his friend. "When will they bury the old man?"

"Who is dead?" Scrooge asked himself. "Why does the Ghost want me to see this? I will look to see what I am doing in this time to come."

The robe fell over Scrooge. When it fell away, Scrooge said, "Look at the crowds of poor people who are living in the streets!" The Ghost pointed to three people pushing through an old door. "They are going to the rag-and-bone man," Scrooge said.

The rag-and-bone man laughed as the three people walked in. "Here are my friends: The charwoman, the laundress, and the undertaker's man!"

"We have good things for you!" said the charwoman. "A dead man does not care what we take!"

"What did you take?" asked the rag-and-bone man.

"I have his bed curtains!" said the charwoman.

"There he was, dead in his bed," laughed the rag-and-bone man. "You walked in to take down his bed curtains?"

"He did not like giving me money for my work when he was living," said the charwoman. "Now he can not stop me from taking his things. What will you give for his shirt?"

The rag-and-bone man held up the shirt. "This is a good shirt!"

"Can you believe they wanted to bury the old man in it?" laughed the charwoman.

As they laughed, the robe fell over Scrooge. Now he was in a room. "There should be a light in here. I can not see! What is this?" Scrooge touched a sheet over a bed. "I can see now. This old sheet is hiding something! It hides the dead man!"

The ghost pointed at the sheet.

"You want me to take the sheet from his face," Scrooge said. "I can not look at his face! I have never seen a man this alone. Who will care when they hear this man is dead?"

The robe fell over Scrooge. He was in a poor family's house. "It is wrong for me to laugh," said the father to the mother. "I am happy he is dead! We should have never borrowed money from the old man. He did not want to give us more time. He wanted to take this house from us!"

"This family is happy to hear a man is dead!" Scrooge said. "People should care! I want to see people who care for the dead!"

The black robe fell over Scrooge. When the robe fell away, Scrooge looked up. "We are at Bob Cratchit's house! Why are we here?"

The Ghost of Christmas Yet to Come

COMPREHENSION CHECK

Preview Answer:
??

Choose the best answer.

1. Scrooge can not see the face of the Ghost because
____a. the night is too dark to see.
____b. his robe is hiding his face.
____c. Scrooge is too afraid to look.
____d. the Ghost does not have a face.

2. When Scrooge sees the men who work near his counting house they are
____a. talking about a man who is dead.
____b. coming out of Fred's house.
____c. on their way home for Christmas.
____d. walking to where they work.

3. The rag-and-bone man
____a. makes toys from things people do not want.
____b. is friendly with the three people who come into his shop.
____c. does this kind of work to keep the streets clean.
____d. has his shop on a pretty street.

4. The laundress, the charwoman, and the undertaker's man
____a. are from the same family.
____b. live at the rag-and-bone man's shop.
____c. want to make the shop look better.
____d. have come with things they have stolen.

5. When the charwoman saw that the man was dead, she
____a. called for a doctor.
____b. walked in to take down his curtains.
____c. ran away because she was afraid.
____d. wanted to help the dead man's family.

6. When he was still living, the dead man
____a. was not nice to the charwoman.
____b. gave a lot of money to the laundress.
____c. was a friend of the charwoman.
____d. told the undertaker's man that he could have the bed curtains.

7. The dead man is in a room
____a. being cared for by the undertaker.
____b. at the rag-and-bone man's shop.
____c. with a strong light over him.
____d. covered by a sheet.

8. When the poor family in the house hears the man is dead they
____a. wish they had borrowed more money from him.
____b. want to go help the dead man's family.
____c. are happy he can not take their home now.
____d. wish the dead man had more time.

9. Another name for this story could be
____a. "The Dead Man."
____b. "The Charwoman Cleans House."
____c. "At the Rag-and-Bone Man's Shop."
____d. "The Black Robe."

10. This story is mainly about
____a. how people should be nice to the charwoman.
____b. Scrooge liking how the rag-and-bone man makes money.
____c. a man who did not care for others will not be cared for himself.
____d. how this ghost is the one Scrooge is the most afraid of.

Check your answers with the keys on page 67.

The Ghost of Christmas Yet to Come

VOCABULARY CHECK

bed	black	take	things	time	who

I. Sentences to Finish
Fill in the blank in each sentence with the correct key word from the box above.

1. _____ do you want to come with us?

2. I will have _____ to help you with your work soon.

3. Mom wants Molly to make her _____ when she gets up.

4. Jared put his _____ away when he came home from school.

5. People say _____ cats are bad luck, but I think they are pretty.

6. Brenda did not want to _____ her hat with her.

II True or False?
Are the sentences true or false? Check one line.

	True	False
1. Brothers are **things**.	____	____
2. A doctor is **who** you see when you are sick.	____	____
3. A **bed** is something you put on your feet to walk.	____	____
4. When you burn food it will turn **black**.	____	____
5. You can **take** money out of your bank.	____	____
6. **Time** is something that floats on water.	____	____

Check your answers with the keys on page 72.

A Changed Man

PREPARATION

Key Words

after	(af´ ter)	at a time following *We are going for a walk <u>after</u> we eat.*
all	(ôl)	the whole of *I can not believe you ate <u>all</u> the food!* every one or every thing *<u>All</u> of us want to go to the party.*
day	(dā)	a time of 24 hours *Can you tell me what <u>day</u> this is?*
hand	(hand)	the part of the arm with fingers *Which <u>hand</u> do you use to hold your knife when you are eating?*
hurry	(her´ ē)	to move quickly *You have to <u>hurry</u> or the bus will go without you.* *The firemen <u>hurried</u> to their truck.*
if	(if)	supposing that *<u>If</u> it snows, we can still go to the park.*

A Changed Man

Necessary Words

clothes	(klōŦHz)	things made out of cloth that are worn to cover one's body *Many people wear black <u>clothes</u> when someone they love has died.*
crazy	(krā' zē)	without good sense; unwise *My cat acts like she is <u>crazy</u> when chasing a string.*
future	(fyü´ chər)	the time to come *Most people do not know what they will be doing in the <u>future</u>.*
grave	(grāv)	a space in the ground that is made for burying a body *Jaye was not afraid until she saw the ghost come out of it's <u>grave</u>.*
need	(nēd)	not able to do without *I will <u>need</u> help to get all the work done.*
sorry	(sor´ ē)	feeling sad or feeling it would be better if something had not happened *Brandon was <u>sorry</u> for taking the last of the cake.*

A Changed Man

At the Cratchits' house, Scrooge sees that Tiny Tim is dead!

> **Preview**   1. Read the name of the story.
> 2. Look at the picture.
> 3. Read the sentence under the picture.
> 4. Read the first (   ) paragraphs of the story.
> 5. Then answer the following question.
>
> *You learned from your preview that Mrs. Cratchit hurts because*
> ____a.   she has been working for so long.
> ____b.   she thinks the family should be helping her more.
> ____c.   she can not see well in the dark.
> ____d.   the black clothing makes her remember that Tim is dead.
>
> *Turn to the Comprehension Check on page 64 for the right answer.*

Now read the story.
Read to find out what Scrooge finds out about the dead man.

A Changed Man

Tiny Tim's mother was working on something black. "It hurts to look on all this black," said his mother.

"Tim's mother is making black clothes," Scrooge said. "Tim is dead!"

Bob looked at the clothes. "Now we will have clothes for the day we bury Tim." He looked at the dead boy on the bed in the next room. "My little boy!"

After a time, Bob stopped crying. "I have seen Scrooge's nephew. He was sorry to hear Tim is dead. He said to come to his house if we need help."

Scrooge looked at the black clothes in the mother's hand. "Who was the dead man alone in the room?" Scrooge asked the Ghost.

The robe fell over Scrooge. Scrooge looked. "There are many graves here."

The Ghost pointed to one grave.

"I will look at the grave after I ask this. If I change, will the future change?" The Ghost pointed to the grave.

Scrooge looked over. "This is my grave! I am the dead man! Why did I have to see the future if I can not change it? I have changed! From now on, Christmas will live in my heart!"

The Ghost pushed Scrooge away. Scrooge did not give up. He held the Ghost's robe. The black robe changed in his hands.

"This is not a robe," Scrooge said. "This is a bed curtain. The charwoman did not take it down! I am living!"

Scrooge looked out his window. A boy was walking down the street. "Boy, what day is this?"

The boy looked at Scrooge as if he believed the old man was crazy. "It is Christmas!"

"The Ghosts changed me in one night!" Scrooge laughed. "Boy, I want you to go get a big goose. I will give you money for it. You will take it to Bob Cratchit's house. Hurry! The faster you go, the more money I will give you!"

Scrooge hurried to his door. "I love you, door knocker!" he said.

On the streets, he looked for the gentleman who wanted help for the poor. "Come see me after Christmas," Scrooge said to the gentleman. "I will give all I can!"

Scrooge hurried to Fred's house. "I am sorry for what I said."

Taking Scrooge's hand in his, Fred said, "Come in!" When the day ended, all of his family were so happy that Scrooge had helped them.

The day after Christmas, Scrooge hurried to his counting house. Bob walked in after the time he should have.

"You did not come to work when you should have!" Scrooge said.

"I am sorry," Bob said.

"You do not like the money I give you." Scrooge laughed. "I will have to give you more!"

"Scrooge is crazy!" Bob said to himself.

Scrooge helped Tim, who lived through many more Christmases. Scrooge liked to give away money. People believed he was crazy. Scrooge did not care. His heart laughed, and this was all he needed. We should all love Christmas as Scrooge did. As Tiny Tim said, "God Bless us, Every One!"

A Changed Man

COMPREHENSION CHECK

Choose the best answer.

1. Tim's mother is making black clothes for
____a. when they bury Tim.
____b. the dead man on the bed.
____c. Bob to wear when he works at the counting house.
____d. when they go to see Scrooge's nephew.

2. Scrooge's nephew wanted
____a. to go see Topper get married.
____b. to tell Bob that Scrooge was dead.
____c. Bob to come to him if his family needed help.
____d. to take over Scrooge's counting house.

3. After they leave the Cratchits' house, the Ghost takes Scrooge to
____a. his counting house.
____b. see Scrooge's grave.
____c. the dead man's room.
____d. Fred's house.

4. Scrooge wants to believe that
____a. the Ghost will change the future for him.
____b. he can change the future if he changes himself.
____c. Belle will come back and he will marry her.
____d. he will never have to die.

5. The Ghost's robe changes into
____a. the charwoman.
____b. Scrooge's shirt.
____c. the black clothes of the Cratchit family.
____d. the bed curtains around Scrooge's bed.

6. Scrooge wants the boy in the street to
____a. take a big goose to the Cratchits' house.
____b. take a big goose to his nephew's house.
____c. help him find the gentleman.
____d. give food to the poor.

7. People believe Scrooge is crazy because he
____a. laughed when Bob was not on time for work.
____b. told people about the ghosts.
____c. changed from loving money to giving it away.
____d. danced at Fred's house.

8. Scrooge changes the way he lives and
____a. stops working at his counting house.
____b. gives his house to Fred.
____c. saves Tiny Tim.
____d. helps the ghosts help other people.

9. Another name for this story could be
____a. "The End of Tiny Tim."
____b. "Scrooge Saves Himself."
____c. "Scrooge and Fred."
____d. "Giving up the Ghosts."

10. This story is mainly about
____a. Scrooge changing his life for the better.
____b. the Cratchit family helping Scrooge.
____c. Marley's ghost becoming free of his chains.
____d. three ghosts coming to help Scrooge.

Check your answers with the keys on page 67.
This page may be reproduced for classroom use.

A Changed Man

VOCABULARY CHECK

after	all	day	hand	hurry	if

I. Sentences to Finish
Fill in the blank in each sentence with the correct key word from the box above.

1. June held the kitten in one _____.

2. What _____ should we go to the zoo?

3. Jody is coming to the house _____ school.

4. I will take the dogs home _____ Charles can not.

5. _____ of the candy is in the jar.

6. Trina has to _____ to get to school in time.

II. Using the Words
On the lines below, write six of your own sentences using the keywords from the box above. Use each word once, drawing a line under the key word.

1. _____

2. _____

3. _____

4. _____

5. _____

6. _____

Check your answers with the keys on page 72.
This page may be reproduced for classroom use.

NOTES

COMPREHENSION CHECK PROGRESS CHART
Lessons: CTR A-91 to CTR A-100

LESSON NUMBER	QUESTION NUMBER										PAGE NUMBER
	1	2	3	4	5	6	7	8	9	10	
CTR-110-91	d	(c)	d	a	b	d	c	a	△c	[b]	10
CTR-110-92	a	c	c	d	b	a	a	(d)	△c	[d]	16
CTR-110-93	b	c	a	d	(b)	a	d	d	△b	[a]	22
CTR-110-94	a	c	b	(a)	d	c	b	c	△a	[b]	28
CTR-110-95	d	d	(a)	b	b	c	a	(d)	△c	[d]	34
CTR-110-96	a	c	b	(a)	c	b	b	c	△d	[d]	40
CTR-110-97	a	(a)	c	c	b	d	b	(d)	△d	[a]	46
CTR-110-98	b	d	a	a	b	d	(c)	c	△a	[b]	52
CTR-110-99	b	a	b	(d)	b	a	d	c	△a	[c]	58
CTR-110-100	a	c	b	b	d	a	(c)	c	△b	[a]	64

◯ = Inference (not said straight out, but you know from what is said)

△ = Another name for the story

☐ = Main idea of the story

VOCABULARY CHECK ANSWER KEY
Lessons: CTR A-91 to CTR A-92

LESSON NUMBER			PAGE NUMBER

91. ALONE FOR CHRISTMAS   11

   I.   1. money
           2. give
           3. are
           4. there
           5. alone
           6. his

   II.   1. NO
           2. YES
           3. NO
           4. NO
           5. YES
           6. YES

92. MARLEY'S GHOST   17

   I.   1. walk
           2. door
           3. Why
           4. friend
           5. was
           6. hear

   II.   1. why   a. hear
           2. hear   b. was
           3. door   c. friend
           4. was   d. walk
           5. friend   e. door
           6. walk   f. Why

LESSON NUMBER		PAGE NUMBER

93.   **GHOSTS IN THE NIGHT**   **23**

I.
1. three
2. window
3. next
4. when
5. one
6. night

II.

```
        ²W
 ¹N  I  G  H  T
        E
     ³W  I  N  ⁴O  W
           N
        ⁵N  E  X  ⁶T
                 H
                 E
                 R
                 E
```

94.   **THE GHOST OF CHRISTMAS PAST**   **29**

I.
1. girl
2. school
3. am
4. boy
5. light
6. man

II.
1. school
2. girl
3. light
4. am
5. man
6. boy

LESSON NUMBER		PAGE NUMBER

95. LOVE FOR BELLE 35

I.
1. woman
2. be
3. laugh
4. more
5. cry
6. her

II.

```
 B   R   A   W   E
 E   E   R   O   M
 M   H   L   M   Y
 H   G   U   A   L
 C   R   Y   N   R
```

The name of the first ghost to visit Scrooge was M A R L E Y.

96. THE GHOST OF CHRISTMAS PRESENT 41

I.
1. than
2. room
3. over
4. many
5. street
6. never

II.
1. room
2. never
3. than
4. many
5. street
6. over

VOCABULARY CHECK ANSWER KEY
Lessons: CTR A-97 to CTR A-98

    I.   1. us
            2. every
            3. live
            4. as
            5. from
            6. people

    II.   1. from
            2. as
            3. every
            4. people
            5. us
            6. live

Answer to the cryptogram: SHE WANTS MARTHA TO COME HOME.

    I.   1. thcy
            2. happy
            3. ask
            4. your
            5. old
            6. does

    II.   1. she   **53**
            2. this
            3. never
            4. over
            5. kitten
            6. light

VOCABULARY CHECK ANSWER KEY
Lessons: CTR A-99 to CTR A-100

LESSON NUMBER			PAGE NUMBER
99.	**THE GHOST OF CHRISTMAS YET TO COME**		**59**

    I.
1. who
2. time
3. bed
4. things
5. black
6. take

    II.
1. False
2. True
3. False
4. True
5. True
6. False

LESSON NUMBER			PAGE NUMBER
100.	**A CHANGED MAN**		**65**

    I.
1. hand
2. day
3. after
4. if
5. all
6. hurry